Maggie and the Chocolate War

Maggie and the Chocolate War

Michelle Mulder

Second Story Press

LIBRARY AND ARCHIVES CANADA CATALOGUING IN PUBLICATION

Mulder, Michelle
Maggie and the chocolate war / by Michelle Mulder.

(Kids' power series)
ISBN 978-1-897187-27-2

1. Strikes and lockouts—Chocolate industry—Juvenile fiction. I. Title.
II. Series.

PS8626.U435M33 2007   jC813'.6   C2007-903519-1

Edited by Gena Gorrell
Cover and text design by Melissa Kaita

Printed and bound in Canada

Second Story Press gratefully acknowledges the support of the Ontario Arts Council and the Canada Council for the Arts for our publishing program. We acknowledge the financial support of the Government of Canada through the Book Publishing Industry Development Program.

Canada Council   Conseil des Arts
for the Arts   du Canada

ONTARIO ARTS COUNCIL
CONSEIL DES ARTS DE L'ONTARIO

Published by
SECOND STORY PRESS
20 Maud Street, Suite 401
Toronto, Ontario, Canada
M5V 2M5
www.secondstorypress.ca

Contents

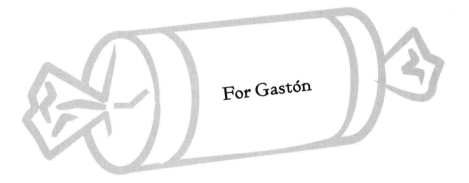

For Gastón

Chapter 1
Maggie's Secret Plan

"Be careful," Maggie's father said, putting Mrs. Bates's package into the bike basket.

"Of course I will," said Maggie. "After all the time I spent convincing Mom to let me do this, I'm not going to mess it up now!" In 1947, usually only boys delivered groceries, but Maggie would prove that she could do just as good a job.

It was a Saturday in late April. Here in Victoria, British Columbia, the weather was warmer than in the rest of Canada, but the mornings were still chilly. Maggie had on her favorite yellow dress (which didn't look a bit like the curtains her mother had made it from), the itchy brown stockings that her mother insisted she wear, and Thomas's old leather shoes. She was ready for anything! She tore off down the street, pedaling as fast as she could.

When she got to the corner, she smiled to see Mrs. Morrison's front yard full of bright yellow tulips, and she waved to Mr. Garnet, who was mowing his lawn. "Nice bike," he called out.

"Thank you," she called back. It was her brother's old bike, actually. He had gotten it a few Christmases ago, during the war against Hitler, when people could still afford to buy things. Lately, everything was getting so expensive that her family couldn't even afford meat for dinner anymore, never mind a bicycle for Maggie. She didn't mind much, though. Thomas's bike was only a little too big for her, and she liked the little basket that her dad had put on the back. A new bike would cost ten dollars, and that was a lot of money—as much as fifty trips to the movies. As much as *two hundred* chocolate bars!

Chocolate was the main reason that Maggie had become her father's delivery girl. Her best friend, Josephine had never ever had a chocolate bar all to herself. (She had six brothers and sisters who always wanted to share.) Jo's birthday was just six days away. Maggie's father had promised her one penny for every two deliveries she made, so if Maggie made ten deliveries before Jo's birthday, she could buy her friend a five-cent candy bar that Jo wouldn't have to share with anybody. Maggie could already imagine her friend's crooked-toothed grin, and her waving hands, as she told everyone that Maggie was the Best Friend Ever.

Maggie soared happily down the hill, past the big houses, to the brown-brick neighborhood where Mrs. Bates lived.

Maggie had never met Mrs. Bates, but she knew this neighborhood well. On Sundays, her dad's store was closed, and when the weather was good, she and her parents walked this way to the harbor. They liked to watch the fancy yachts float toward the big, gray Legislature Buildings toward the ivy-covered Empress Hotel, where kings, queens, and movie stars stayed. Halfway down this block, a golden cocker spaniel always ran out to greet visitors, and her father often brought a stick for the dog to play with.

But today, as Maggie turned onto Mrs. Bates's street, the bouncing, barking dog ran right in front of her bike.

"Stop!" Maggie shouted, and squeezed hard on her handbrakes. The dog darted away just in time, but the brown-paper package in Maggie's basket went flying over her head and landed with a splat on the pavement. The dog sniffed it, tail wagging.

"Oh no! Now what am I going to do?" Maggie cried. She'd been a delivery girl for only ten minutes, and already she had made such a mess! She would have to go home with this slimy, dripping package of six broken eggs. Forty-six cents a dozen, her mother had said. Maggie had smashed twenty-three cents' worth. That would be forty-six deliveries, to pay her father back! With so many foods in short supply—not just meat, but sugar and butter and candy—wasting food seemed like about the worst thing she could do. They were already eating porridge twice a day, and turning curtains into clothing. Things would be even worse after an expensive accident like this.

She couldn't bear to think of the disappointed look that would be on her father's face.

Chapter 2
The Chocolate Shelf

A pile of bicycles lay outside her father's shop when Maggie returned. Through the window, she saw a crowd of children huddled around the chocolate-bar shelf.

Many adults shopped downtown, because the stores there were bigger and sold more things, but the neighborhood kids always came to her dad's store for candy. His selection was as good as anyone else's, and the prices were the same. He knew everyone's favorites, and sometimes he even told adults that he was sold out before he really was, just so the kids wouldn't be disappointed by an empty chocolate shelf.

Maggie was proud to have a father everyone knew and liked. She just wished all those kids weren't there right now.

She wheeled the bicycle around back and lifted the dripping package from her little basket. On second thought, she put it back and wiped her hand clean on the only remaining patch of grass. Her mother had turned all the rest of the yard into a vegetable garden, in her never-ending struggle to reduce the grocery bill.

Maggie snuck into the back of the shop. Normally, she loved the store: the smell of the dark wooden floors and cabinets; the colorful jars of candies lining the shelves all the way to the ceiling; the straight rows of canned peas, carrots, and potatoes; the loaves of Aunt Marjorie's fresh bread in the basket by the till. And the very best part was the little shelf just below the cash register—the chocolate-bar shelf, where all the kids were huddled now.

Maggie's father glanced up from behind the counter and smiled at her, but his smile vanished when he saw the look on her face. He said something to the children and hurried to the back of the store. Of course, this made all the kids turn and look.

"Hi Maggie," Jeffrey Johnson called. Jeffrey was her brother's best friend. He was taller than Thomas, with sandy hair and freckles, and he wore glasses in thick brown frames. When he wasn't upstairs trading hockey cards with Thomas, he was here in front of the chocolate shelf, carefully deciding how to spend the nickel his parents gave him whenever he asked. His father had a good job at the bank. Maggie had never seen Jeffrey in second-hand clothes, and he was one of the few who could buy as many candy bars as he wanted, but at least he shared. Maggie liked him because he never treated her like a kid.

A few of the other kids smiled at her, but many of them were too deep in their candy discussion to turn her way. "I'll get that one, and you get one with almonds, and we'll split them both, okay?"

"But I don't like all the nuts and stuff. I just want *chocolate*. And this one's bigger than that one, don't you think?"

Maggie's father ignored the chatter and put a hand on her shoulder. "What is it?" he asked. "You look like you've seen a ghost."

"Not a ghost," Maggie whispered back miserably. "A *dog*. Too late. I used my brakes, but the eggs went flying and landed all over everything, and Mom says they're forty-six cents a dozen, so I broke twenty-three cents' worth, and—" She stopped herself before she could tell him about the surprise for Josephine. She didn't want him to feel sorry for her and just *give* her the candy bar. Her idea was to buy it, to earn it, just the way an adult had to. That was what would make her the Best Friend Ever. If only she hadn't broken the eggs!

"It could have happened to anyone," her dad said, but his eyes looked much more disappointed than his words sounded. She would have done anything to take that sad look off his face.

"I'll pay you back. I promise," she said.

"I know you will," he told her. "I'll wrap up six more eggs." He squeezed her hand, and a few minutes later Maggie was on her way again.

The second time she left the shop, Maggie rode as though excitable dogs might be lurking around every corner, and her deliveries took twice as long as she'd hoped. By the time she had finished her last one, the sun was high in the sky, and her stomach was growling. She trudged up the stairs to their apartment over the shop. Thomas's old shoes felt even heavier than usual.

When she opened the apartment door, the radio was playing loudly in the kitchen, and her mother stood barefoot, her white apron tied around her waist, a scrub brush in one hand. "What do you mean the price of butter is going up?" she demanded of the radio. "What's the use of ending rationing if the prices rise higher than anyone can afford?" She shook her head in frustration and got down on her knees to scrub the floor.

Maggie knew what her mother meant. During the war, they had needed special ration tickets to buy things like meat and

By 1947, war rationing had ended, but the cost of food continued to climb. Some shopkeepers tried to keep prices under control.

Vegetables were plentiful, but they cost more than ever.

butter, and they hadn't been allowed to buy very much. Now the ration tickets were gone, but prices were shooting up, and people got even less than before. Maggie could see why her mother was mad. Still, if she could yell at a radio, what would she say about all those broken eggs?

"Mom?"

Her mother looked at her and laughed in surprise. "How long have you been standing there?"

Maggie was about to respond when there was a knock on the back door.

"Mercy," her mother said, pulling the kerchief from her head and trying to straighten her flyaway hair. "Maggie, you get washed up for lunch. I'll see who that is."

Maggie followed orders. When she came back, Jo's mother, Mrs. Martin, was sitting on the sofa. "The blue will go perfectly with Jo's eyes," she was telling Maggie's mother. "Oh, hello, Maggie. I hear you've become your father's delivery girl. How is it going?"

Maggie avoided her eyes. "All right, I guess. I'm all done for the day."

Her mother smiled and asked Maggie to warm up the soup on the stove and set the table. "And please move that blue dress over to the counter. Mrs. Martin wants me to rework it for Josephine."

"It's for her birthday," Mrs. Martin said, as if Maggie couldn't guess. "We saved for ages to get her a new dress, but we really couldn't afford it, and then the lady I work for offered me this one. I'd redo it myself, but someone at home is bound to find out. I want this to be a surprise. You won't tell Jo, will you, Maggie?"

Maggie shook her head and added one more secret to her collection. She knew Jo would love the new dress. Usually, Jo's clothes were hand-me-downs from her three older sisters, and they were faded and frayed. One time, when Maggie was visiting, she helped Jo dye a white dress yellow with onion skins, just for variety. Over the years of the war, with all the shortages and rationing, people had learned all kinds of ways to make something from nothing.

After Mrs. Martin left, Maggie's mother danced into the kitchen where Maggie was setting the table. "You helped me get a job, Miss Maggie Jenkins! Josephine's mother asked me to make the dress because she loves how I made your yellow one."

Maggie laughed. "Can you make something this beautiful from a real dress, instead of curtains?" she teased.

"I'll do my best."

Together they finished heating the soup and setting the table. Then Maggie took a deep breath and told her mother about the eggs. "I'm really sorry, Mom. I promised to pay Dad back."

"I'm sure you will, dear." She ruffled Maggie's hair, and Maggie's worries faded. Maybe her dad would let her buy the candy bar first, before she paid for the eggs. She smiled to herself, imagining once more Jo's surprised face when she opened the present.

Maggie had just put the last glass of water on the table when Thomas burst in from outside. "I can't believe it!" he shouted, letting the apartment door slam behind him and tossing his baseball mitt on the floor with a *whoomp*. "They're raising the price of *chocolate*!"

Chapter 3
Hey, Have You Heard?

"Have you heard? Can you believe it?" Jo arrived at the beach running, waving an envelope in her hand. Her littlest brother, Will, ran behind her as fast as his legs could carry him. Their white-blond hair shone in the sun.

"Heard what?" Maggie had heard far too many things already that day: Thomas's complaints about porridge at breakfast that morning, the splat of twenty-three cents worth of eggs on the street, and, to crown it all, Thomas's terrible announcement right before lunch. Whatever Jo was talking about seemed to be in the envelope she was waving, though, and Maggie couldn't imagine what that contained.

"Have you heard about the candy-bar prices?"

"Someone sent you a letter about it?" Maggie asked.

"No, the letter's from my cousin, but on the way here I saw Gladys, and she says five-cent candy bars are going to cost eight cents! That's almost double!"

"I *know*." Maggie groaned. "How can anyone afford chocolate now?"

Jo shook her head, and her hair swished around her face. "Even Gladys won't be able to buy much anymore. Can you believe she gets five cents a week to do whatever she wants with? Anyway, even with all that money, she'll have to save her allowance for two weeks to buy a candy bar."

Little Will caught up, panting. "Candy bar? Can I have some?"

"Nope," Jo said. "That's one thing you won't be having for a long, long time."

"One day," Will said, "I'm going to make a hundred dollars, and I'll buy chocolate bars for our whole family, and for Maggie, too. I'll buy a hundred Hersheys, and a hundred Dairy Milk, and a hundred..."

Maggie smiled. Why couldn't she have a sweet little brother like Will, instead of smelly, cranky old Thomas?

"No one has a hundred dollars, silly," Jo said. "And if they did, they certainly wouldn't spend it on candy bars." She wiped her brother's runny nose with a handkerchief. Little Will's nose was always running, and he always forgot his hanky, but Jo carried extras in her pockets. Maggie had better remind her mother about the importance of pockets on the secret birthday dress. At least Jo would have one nice present. Maggie's chocolate-bar dream seemed very far off now.

Will jumped down the stairs to the sand, and Jo and Maggie followed. "Who decides these things, anyway?" Maggie asked.

"The government, I think," Jo said. "Mom says that during the war, the government gave money to companies that make things like butter and sugar, so prices rose really slowly. Otherwise people couldn't afford to eat. But now the government isn't giving out so much money, so the companies are raising the prices. I guess the government thinks we can afford everything just fine now."

Maggie rolled her eyes. "That's ridiculous."

"I know," Jo said. Then she remembered the envelope in her hand. "My cousin Annette is coming to stay with us for the summer, because both her parents are going north to work, just to make ends meet! They're going to get good summer jobs with logging camps that pay a lot of money."

Maggie had a sick feeling in her stomach. "Is that what the letter says?" Annette had stayed for a few weeks the summer before, and Maggie had barely seen Jo the whole time. And after Annette left, all Jo could talk about was how great Annette was.

Tall, strong, fastest runner, best rope jumper, best storyteller....
Maggie had got so tired of Annette's "bests" last year that she
didn't ever want to see her again. Why did she have to show up
now and take up all of Jo's time?

"She's staying *all* summer?" asked Maggie, picking up a mussel shell. She tossed it at a boulder, cracking the shell in two.

Jo didn't seem to notice how mad Maggie was. "It's going to
be great!" she said.

A long time passed before the waves that licked their toes
washed away Maggie's bad mood, but eventually she decided
not to be grumpy about the eggs, or the price of chocolate, or
Annette. There was no point being grumpy while Jo was still
her best friend. The eggs were already broken. And there was
nothing any kid could do about the price of chocolate, right?

◁▷ ◁▷ ◁▷

"We have to do *something*," Jeffrey said.

Maggie, Jo, and Will had been returning home through
Beacon Hill Park, their pockets full of pearly clam and mussel
shells, when they saw Jeffrey on his bicycle. He had stopped and
asked if they'd heard the news.

"Of course. Everyone in Victoria has heard by now," Maggie
said.

"We should complain," Jeffrey said. "When adults get mad, people listen. Why shouldn't they listen to kids?"

Jo laughed. "Tell that to my dad. He says kids should be seen and not heard. How can you get mad silently?"

Maggie couldn't imagine Jo's six brothers and sisters being silent *ever*, especially when they were mad.

"What about making signs and carrying them in a protest march?" Jeffrey asked. "That's what some mothers did when

Women protesting rising prices picketed in front of government buildings, hoping politicians would take up their cause.

the price of milk went up. They went downtown and spent all morning marching in front of the Legislature Buildings where the government works."

"Did the price of milk go down again?" asked Maggie.

"Not yet, but people say it has to." Jeffrey crossed his arms over his chest and shook his head. "It'll be the same with chocolate, I think. Who's going to spend eight whole cents on a candy bar? It's just not right."

Jo jumped up and down, the way she did before a parade, or when she was allowed to sleep over at Maggie's. "I think we *should* protest. My mom says it's the only way to tell the government what we think. And in Social Studies last week, Mrs. Sampson said it's our right as citizens to tell the government how we feel."

Maggie thought it was a great idea. And it was something she and Jo could do as a team. "If we get lots of kids together and make lots of noise, they'll have to listen to us! I have paints we can use, and I'm sure Dad has lots of extra cardboard boxes. We'll make enormous signs—lots of them, all with different messages! And we'll go up and down the streets, waving them. We'll really tell them what we think!" She had no idea whether they could bring the price back down, but it was worth a shot. The Best Friend Ever present depended on it.

"We have to tell every kid we know," said Jeffrey. "And *fast*."

Chapter 4
Kids Unite!

"The kids in Chemainus and Ladysmith are already protesting," Thomas said. "The newspaper said they made signs, and they were marching in front of the stores that charge eight cents for a candy bar."

Twenty-four hours had passed since Maggie had first learned about the rise in chocolate prices. Word was traveling fast. Now, on Sunday afternoon, fifteen kids had gathered in front of her father's store to talk about protesting.

"My mother," said Jeffrey, "was talking to her cousin on the telephone yesterday."

The children turned and paid him their full attention. Not everyone had a telephone, and most of the children had never talked on one.

"She said some teenagers in Chemainus drove all over town, protesting and shouting, *Down with eight-cent bars!*"

"Kids everywhere are fighting the price hike now," said Thomas.

"We should go to Ottawa and tell the government what we think!" shouted another boy, raising a fist in the air.

"Frank," Jeffrey said, "how will we get all the way to Ottawa when we can't even afford an eight-cent candy bar?"

"It was just a thought."

Thomas rubbed his hands together. He'd been secretive about his plan, refusing to tell

The Daily Colonist,
April 25, 1947, front page

Social Editor .... Empire 3311

NO. 113—EIGHTY-NINTH YEAR

Price of Candy Brings Strike Of Youngsters

Up-Island Children Oppose Increase In Added Cost of Candy Bars

(Special to The Colonist)

CHEMAINUS, April 24.—Children of Chemainus and Ladysmith went on a "chocolate bar" strike today, and present indications are that the boycott will speedily spread to Duncan, Cobble Hill, Nanaimo, Parksville, Qualicum Beach, Courtenay, Comox, Campbell River, Alberni and Port Alberni.

"Chocolate bars were not worth six cents, but at eight cents we think we are being robbed," a teen-aged girl commented at Chemainus.

"What are you going to do without chocolate bars?" a reporter asked a Ladysmith boy.

"Ice cream's better," he grinned.

Store clerks at both Chemainus and Ladysmith disclosed that no children purchased chocolate bars today, despite adequate supplies and tempting counter displays. However, many sales were made to adults, hungry for sweets that have reposed under counters for several years.

Ladysmith reported several cases of adults being "picketed" by children when they emerged from shops with 8-cent "inflation" chocolate bars. Hoots, jeers and sundry uncomplimentary remarks made many a grown-up uncomfortably aware that it would have been better policy to support the children's boycott.

Children of all ages at Chemainus and Ladysmith pinned neatly printed cards on their dresses and jackets bearing the following words:

"Let the penny-pinchers have theirs. We want nickel bars."

"Before, you asked for bars on your knees. Now they throw them in your face."

"Don't be a sucker. Don't buy 8-cent bars."

"Bars are smaller. We won't buy 8-cent bars."

Placards expressing similar sentiments were also tacked up in the business sections of Chemainus and Ladysmith.

Chemainus and Ladysmith Teen Towns are wholeheartedly supporting the chocolate bar boycott.

Pensions Bill Due On Monday

Practical Answer Aim of Legislation

OTTAWA, April 24 (CP).—Health Minister Martin announced tonight in the Commons the Government will introduce its old age pension legislation Monday.

Rising at the conclusion of a short debate on orders in council dealing with old age pensions and attached to the Government's main control bill, Mr. Martin said the Government had given "a great deal of thought" to the old age pension bill, which will increase the current pension rates.

The legislation would not meet the point of view of all members in the House but it would represent the Government's attempt to "deal with this problem as practically as possible in the light of all obligations."

Basic old age pensions now amount $20 a month. A $5 per month supplement was provided for by orders in council. Some provinces also paid a $5 supplement and British Columbia recently increased its amount to $10, making the possible maximum pension there $35.

Maggie anything beyond the fact that it was brilliant. Thomas always thought he was brilliant. Maggie didn't usually agree, but she listened anyway.

"As soon as the prices go up," Thomas said, "we have to start a boycott. We all have to *stop buying chocolate.*"

"What?" Maggie was here because she *wanted* to buy chocolate! She glanced at Jo to see if she understood any of this, but her friend's eyes were wide and disbelieving.

"He's right," said Jeffrey, pushing his glasses back on his freckled nose. "If no one's buying any candy bars, the shopkeepers will *have* to sell them cheaper, just to get rid of them."

Maggie imagined buying Jo's birthday chocolate a month late because of the boycott, and she groaned. Thomas shot her a warning look. "It's the only way," he said to her.

"We'll make big signs," he continued, "and a few kids outside every candy store will tell everyone that they shouldn't buy chocolate."

Maggie frowned. The chocolate-bar shelf was the only part of her father's store that *always* drew customers. If kids outside were protesting and driving customers away, Maggie's parents would worry even more about money. Her mother would yell louder at the radio. They would have to eat *more* porridge.

"Isn't this exciting?" Jo whispered in Maggie's ear. "Imagine! Our very own protest!"

"I don't know," Maggie said. "Won't the shopkeepers get mad? I mean, it's not their fault the prices are going up."

Jo wrinkled her nose. "You mean you're not going to join in?"

"Of course I'll join," Maggie said, not wanting to lose her friend any sooner than necessary. "I just feel bad for the shopkeepers."

Jo shrugged. "Adults will still buy other things at the stores. Anyway, I don't know about you, but I wouldn't break the boycott even if someone *gave* me an eight-cent candy bar."

Maggie winced. Thomas clapped his hands and asked if there were any questions. Jo looked at Maggie, and Maggie looked at Thomas with her lips clamped shut. There was no point trying to talk to him now, in front of all these people. She shook her head and watched as her brother took down names for protest shifts.

"I can go every lunch hour," shouted one kid.

"And I'm free after school. Oh, except Thursdays. That's my piano lesson."

"I can go *during* school," shouted someone else, and everyone laughed.

"It's not Dad's fault," Maggie told Thomas later, when they were sprinkling baking soda on their toothbrushes at the bathroom sink. (Baking soda was cheaper than toothpaste, their mother said.) "You know he can't sell things any cheaper than he does already."

Thomas sighed as though she were too stupid for words. "This isn't about Dad," he said. "Sure, the shopkeepers are caught in the middle, but this is the only way to show the candy-makers how we feel. *They're* the ones raising the prices."

"Then why punish Dad?" Maggie asked.

"We're not punishing him," Thomas said and narrowed his eyes at her. "Don't tell me you're going to keep buying chocolate and ruin everything."

Maggie shook her head. Jo wouldn't eat a chocolate bar during the boycott, even if it was for her birthday. Maggie would just have to think of another present. Meanwhile, though, she was worried about her father. He would feel horrible having people march in front of his store as if he'd done something wrong. He'd lose money, too, if no one bought any chocolate.

Why didn't Thomas understand what a boycott would mean? He was always complaining because they couldn't afford things like meat and lots of bread, and they wound up eating porridge twice a day sometimes, because it was cheap. "Are you ready to eat *more* porridge," Maggie asked him, "if we drive away Dad's customers and we can't afford anything else?"

Thomas's answer surprised her. "Maggie, this is important. Sometimes, you've got to sacrifice something."

She jabbed her toothbrush into her mouth, not wanting to talk anymore. Why couldn't he sacrifice his complaining early in the mornings, then? Wasn't their parents' happiness important? Big brothers were just so stupid sometimes.

That night, Maggie had trouble sleeping. When her parents went to bed, she heard their conversation through the wall.

"I've made a decision," her mother said, and silence swelled before she spoke again. "Janet Martin and I are joining the housewives' collective."

Maggie pressed her ear closer to the wall and wondered whether Jo knew about this. What was the housewives' collective, anyway?

"Maggie found me yelling at the radio yesterday," her mother continued. "Last week, it was because the price of butter was going up. The week before, it was meat. I'm sick of always yelling with no one to hear. The collective is organizing a protest."

Maggie's dad sighed. "It won't get you anywhere." His voice

was low, tense, and controlled, the way it had been when he found Maggie cutting pictures out of his favorite magazine for a school project the year before. "The government isn't going to listen to a bunch of angry women."

"It worked in Regina," Mother said. "The collective complained so much that the prices came down again."

"That won't last."

Maggie wished this conversation would stop, but her mother kept going. "The women must feel a whole lot better about themselves in the meantime." She laughed. "At least they're doing something besides yelling at the radio."

Maggie's father's voice rumbled in a reply that Maggie couldn't make out. She pulled away from the wall, not wanting to hear any more. For what seemed like hours, she tried to conjure up dreams in which her father was happy *and* Jo had her own five-cent candy bar. She herself would have a speedy, new bike with a big, padded basket for fragile things and a noisy horn to keep dogs away, and she would make so much money that she and Jo could buy chocolate bars every week, no matter how much adults argued about prices.

Chapter 5
The Best Kind of Grown-Up

"I bet Mrs. Sampson will help with the protest," Jo told Maggie at recess on Monday. "Remember when the school picnic got canceled because of the rain?"

"Yeah." Maggie frowned just as their teacher had, and she wagged her finger at Jo and mimicked the teacher's voice. "Complaining inside a classroom isn't going to help, children. Tell people how you feel. Get the picnic rescheduled."

And with Mrs. Sampson's help, the class did just that. The picnic was held two weeks later, and it was the best one ever, with more sweets than usual and even a little dish of ice cream for everybody.

"Let's talk to her when the bell rings," Jo said. "You'll come with me, won't you?"

"Of course," said Maggie. "I don't want to have to be a millionaire to afford a chocolate bar."

"What about your dad getting mad?"

Maggie shrugged. "He seems mad about a lot of things these days. Last night, he was mad at Mom because she said she was going to protest too."

"Your mother's protesting about chocolate bars?" Jo shouted, then covered her mouth when everyone on the playground stopped to look at her.

Maggie laughed. "Not about chocolate bars, silly. About butter. And flour, and eggs, and everything else."

"Oh. Well, your mother's pretty nifty anyway," Jo said. "And I'm glad you're still going to protest. After the meeting yesterday, I thought you were going to miss out on everything."

"And never have chocolate again?" said Maggie. "Are you kidding? Dad's mad because he's afraid no one will buy anything from him anymore, and we'll be broke. But we *have* to get the price of chocolate down somehow." *Preferably before your birthday,* Maggie thought.

As soon as the bell rang after recess, Maggie slipped her arm through Jo's, and they dashed into class, headed for the big desk in front of the blackboard. Mrs. Sampson was wearing a red dress with little white flowers, and that was the only color in the room. The desks were all beige and black. The posters were black and white. The blackboard was—of course—black. And then there was Mrs. Sampson.

She sat at her desk with her head bent over a stack of math corrections. Her hair was white, and she was so old that most *parents* had had her as a teacher. Maggie's dad said she was the best teacher the city had ever seen. She never used the strap on children, the way other teachers did. "If I don't show you respect, how can I expect you to respect me?" she always asked.

Her skin was as wrinkled as a tortoise's, but when she smiled— as she often did—none of that seemed to matter. She was smiling now.

"Have you heard about candy bars going up to eight cents?" Jo blurted.

"I did hear. I'm sorry."

"We're organizing a protest," Maggie said.

"Good for you!" Mrs. Sampson clapped her hands together. "Have you made your signs yet? Are you thinking of a petition?"

"Maggie's brother's friends are writing letters," Jo said. "Maggie and I are going to make signs with the younger kids. Do you think we could stay in after school to make them here?"

Mrs. Sampson bit her lip, thinking hard. "I don't think Mr. Paul would understand. He says schools should stay out of politics—as if schools were ever anything *but* political. Anyway," she waved the thought away with one hand, "that's another story. I want to help somehow, but let's not involve the school or the principal."

All three of them thought for a few seconds. Maggie imagined the red paint she'd use for her sign, and she tried not to think of the red of her father's face when he got angry. She pictured him storming out of his shop and whispering at all the children to *go away*. He always whispered when he was really angry. He said it was better to be controlled than to fly off the handle, but Maggie couldn't help thinking that flying off the handle—whatever that meant—would be less scary than his red, red face whispering angrily in hers.

Suddenly, Mrs. Sampson smiled. "What if you made the signs in my backyard this afternoon, at about five o'clock? My house is just around the corner, you know."

Maggie and Jo stared at her, unable to believe that any adult would invite a lot of messy kids into her backyard with big bottles of paint and stacks of cardboard. "You must really like chocolate," Jo said finally.

Mrs. Sampson laughed. "For me, it's not about chocolate. It's about you, making your voices heard. Besides, I'm sure you'll all be very orderly, clever, and efficient, because otherwise no one will respect your protest. Right?"

Jo and Maggie nodded eagerly and agreed to bring along as many children as possible, later that day.

Chapter 6
Signs and Slogans

"Hey, Charlie," Maggie said at lunchtime. Her important news made her brave enough to talk to him, even though he was almost as old as Thomas and was the most popular kid in grade five. She stood as tall as she could and asked, "Have you heard about the chocolate protest? We're all making signs at Mrs. Sampson's house after five o'clock today."

"Really?" Charlie looked impressed, but then he crossed his arms over his chest. "Are you sure you've got that right? I don't want to show up at Mrs. Sampson's door and find out you've made a mistake."

"It's no mistake," Maggie said. "You can ask her yourself. Just spread the word, okay? The more kids, the better."

Next, Maggie spotted Jennifer across the playground. Jennifer was the snootiest girl in grade four. Her father worked for the government, and she lived in a mansion just a few blocks from South Park School. She never invited anyone to her house, except on her birthday, when she invited the whole class, and a servant served ice cream and chocolate cake. Most kids invited her to their birthday parties because she brought big, expensive presents, but Maggie didn't like Jennifer's snootiness, so she generally just ignored her. Today was an exception, though. The protest was too important. She ran to tell Jennifer the plan.

After school, Maggie and Jo's walk home took longer than usual. They stopped to talk to every kid old enough to paint a slogan on a sign. "Bring paints and cardboard and lots of ideas," Maggie told everyone. "The future of chocolate depends on us!"

Maggie was relieved not to have any eggs in her delivery basket that afternoon. She had to pedal like crazy to get all the deliveries done, because she kept stopping to talk to kids along the way. Three boys playing jacks, five playing street hockey, and three girls at a lemonade stand all agreed to be at Mrs. Sampson's that night.

"Now you mind your manners, Maggie Jenkins," her mother told her later, when Maggie stood at the front door with cardboard, string, and a stick for her sign. "You don't want to make a nuisance of yourself."

"But she *invited* us, Mom. She asked us to come and told us to tell the other kids."

"I'm not sure she meant the whole neighborhood, though. I don't want to hear that a hundred kids trampled her roses or dumped paint on her sidewalk." Maggie's mother shook her head. "Mrs. Sampson's always had a lot more nerve than anyone. I sure hope she knows what she's doing."

⋙ ⋙ ⋙

The lawn and the whole sidewalk in front of Mrs. Sampson's cheery blue house were covered with newspapers. "Hurray! Our first sign-makers!" the teacher shouted when she saw Maggie, Jo, and Jo's two youngest brothers hurrying down the street.

Jo introduced Allen and Will to Mrs. Sampson. "I told them they couldn't come because they'd make a mess, but they said they'd just watch. They wanted to see what a teacher's house looked like. Will thought you lived at the school."

Mrs. Sampson chuckled. "I'm glad I don't. That desk would be very uncomfortable for sleeping." She put a hand to her back and pretended to hobble around. The boys giggled, and she

34

winked at them. "You can do more than watch, if you want. Heaven knows we have enough newspaper out here to catch the spills! We also have some old shirts to cover your clothes, if you want." She led them along the path to the side gate and into the backyard. The newspaper went all around the house and even covered some of the rose bushes.

"Welcome, welcome!" shouted a big man on the back porch. His cheeks and nose were rosy, and if he had had a beard and a red suit, he might have been Santa's identical twin. He introduced himself as Mr. Sampson and shook each kid's hand as if they were all grown-ups.

Maggie was so busy looking at the beautiful blue house and the matching blue birdhouse on the fence that she almost forgot her manners. "What can we do to help?" she asked, finally.

"Just relax and get your slogans ready," Mr. Sampson said, just as Charlie and a few other kids arrived with cardboard, sticks, and thumbtacks.

"It should be short and funny. Jokes make people like you more," Charlie was telling one of his friends. They were wearing old shirts so big that they clearly belonged to their fathers. Other parents must have been as nervous about messes as Maggie's mother was.

A tall boy Maggie had seen playing marbles earlier came through the back gate. "We have to remind adults what's important to kids. That's what Mom says," he was explaining to a little girl with black braids.

"I already know what I'm going to write on my sign, and I'm not telling anyone," said Allen. "Where's a paintbrush? When can we start?"

Maggie hadn't decided on her own slogan yet. Maybe she would make two signs and give one to little Will—*Lower prices to 5¢. We are short* and *A fool and his money soon part. Eight cents for a bar is only a start.*

By five-thirty, kids had poured onto Mrs. Sampson's street from all directions. Most of them were Maggie and Jo's age, some a bit younger, and one or two as old as Thomas. When so many kids were painting that they no longer fit in the backyard, they spread out around the house and onto the front walk.

"Don't be a sucker. Don't buy eight-cent bars!" shouted Charlie when he was done.

"What this country needs is a good five-cent candy bar," called out Amy Nelson, the smartest kid in grade four.

"We want five-cent candy bars. Eight cents is going too darn far," declared Jennifer.

Maggie smiled, though it was a big effort to be nice to snooty Jennifer. At first Maggie had wondered why Jennifer had even agreed to come tonight. She had figured it out, though, when Jennifer went around to every kid to offer advice on letter size or wording. She always had to be the center of attention. As usual, everyone ignored her—until she said in a loud, clear voice, "I talked on the telephone to my aunt in New Brunswick today."

They all stared. Even *her* family couldn't afford to talk on the telephone to someone so far away, could they? And why would they let a nine-year-old do the talking? Maggie kept her ears perked while Jennifer babbled on.

"The kids in New Brunswick are pooling all their sugar rations," she said, looking around and meeting every kid's eyes. "They're going to get together to make fudge, so no one has to buy eight-cent bars. Isn't that a great idea?"

Maggie laughed. "Do you really think their parents will give up their expensive sugar for something like that?"

"Of course!" Jo said, turning to her friend. "Lots of adults know this is important. Look at Mrs. Sampson."

"But how many Mrs. Sampsons are there in the world?" Maggie asked.

"Enough," snapped Jennifer. She began painting a new sign—furiously, Maggie thought.

"Thanks, Mrs. Sampson," Maggie and several other kids called, trooping out of her backyard with signs painted in large, thick brushstrokes.

"You're the greatest, Mrs. Sampson!"

"We'll buy you a chocolate bar when we win!"

Mrs. Sampson waved to them from her gate. "Just make me proud!" she called back. "I can't eat chocolate anymore anyway."

"Chocolate! Chocolate! Chocolate!" shrieked Jo's two younger brothers, running toward the school playgrounds. A sign saying *Candy is dandy but 8¢ isn't handy* bounced on little Will's shoulders. Allen held high *8¢ bars: a big bite out of a sweet tooth.*

Maggie felt bouncier than she had since breaking the eggs two days earlier. With so many kids boycotting candy bars, chocolate prices would fall in no time. She wouldn't have to worry about her dad's store anymore, and by Friday she would be able to buy Jo's birthday present and be the Best Friend Ever.

Jo lifted her sign (*Roses are red, violets are blue, we're on strike, why aren't you?*) and followed her brothers to the playground. "Can you imagine talking on the telephone to someone in New Brunswick?" she asked.

Maggie rolled her eyes. "I don't believe it. No one would let a kid do something that expensive."

This boy in Montreal was one of many across the country who
protested the rise in chocolate prices.

It wasn't just city kids who protested. Children in rural areas also made their opinions clear.

"I don't know," Jo said. "Mother says Jennifer's family has more money than they know what to do with. I wish my cousin Annette had a telephone. Then I could talk to her whenever I wanted."

Maggie's stomach felt funny. Jo was almost always talking about her cousin these days. And for the next few weeks, Maggie would have to work almost every day to pay her father back for the eggs. By the time Maggie was free to play after school, Jo would be too busy with horrid Annette to care about Maggie.

"What's so great about Annette, anyway?" she asked. "You said your whole family turns upside down to make space for her, and you have to share your bed the whole time she's here."

"That's the best part!" Jo said. "We tell each other stories all night long, and no one tells us to be quiet because Annette's a guest."

Maggie wished she had cousins who lived nearby. The only person who still told her stories was her father, but his stories always ended at exactly nine o'clock, when he turned out the light and said it was time to go to sleep.

Thomas used to tell her stories too. Once he told her about a ghost that lived in the store, and she screamed, and her parents got mad at him for scaring her. Thomas didn't talk to her for a week, until she hid his hockey cards downstairs where the ghost was supposed to sleep, and he called her a dumb kid and told her that none of his stories were true. They talked to each other after that, but the stories never came back.

"Well," Maggie told Jo, "I'll probably be too busy to spend much time with you when Annette's here, anyway."

Jo looked as if she'd been stung. "You're working in July and August, too?"

"Probably." Maggie didn't think her father would need her much over the summer, but her mother would want her to tend the garden, sweep the apartment, and help with the cooking. It seemed important to tell Jo that *someone* needed Maggie, even if Jo didn't. "And the other thing is, I can't be at the protest right away tomorrow. Dad has some deliveries for me."

Jo frowned. "Again? You're always working now."

"I have those eggs to pay back, remember?"

"You're not going to deliver chocolate bars, are you?"

Maggie laughed. "Can you imagine an adult ordering a chocolate bar for delivery? Even Jennifer's parents wouldn't spend their money on that."

Jo seemed happier then, and they swung on the swings without talking for a while. This boycott had better work, Maggie thought. She still hadn't dreamed up any other present as good as a five-cent candy bar, so if the price of chocolate didn't come down, Maggie would never be the Best Friend Ever—and who knew what would happen when Annette arrived?

Time was running out. Only three days were left before Jo's birthday.

Not only Jo's present, but the entire friendship, seemed to depend on how loudly Maggie rallied for the five-cent candy bar.

Chapter 7
Protesting the Protest

Maggie ran home from school on Tuesday afternoon, anxious to escape with her deliveries before the protesters came to force her dad's customers away. Many kids had protested at lunch already, but her father's store was a twenty-minute walk from the nearest school, so the kids hadn't had time to get there during lunch hour. He would see his first batch of angry children in just a few minutes.

She filled her basket with the groceries and took off on her bicycle like a shot. No one had ordered eggs that day, so she rode faster than usual. But after a few deliveries, she had to return to pick up the rest of the orders, and she couldn't avoid the protesters any longer. They waved at her from the front steps of the store. She recognized Charlie from grade five, snooty Jennifer, and a few kids from grade two. She waved back at them and tried to read all their signs without crashing into anything.

8¢ bars can go to hang.
I'm one of the gang.

8¢ bars are now a crime,
in six months time they'll want a dime.

Bar the 8¢ Bar.

The same slogans that had made her so happy the day before made her squirm now when she thought of her father all alone inside his shop. Was he angry? Disappointed? Sad? Did he understand that this had nothing to do with him, as Thomas had said?

"Do you know anything about this, Maggie?" her father asked, when she came through the back door to pick up her last two deliveries. A knot formed in her stomach. He pushed the two packages across the counter for her, and she was still trying to figure out how to answer him when the front door flew open, sending the chimes dancing and tinkling.

"Don't worry," the woman told the children clamoring outside. "I'm buying bread, not chocolate."

Those who had bikes rode around with their signs to help
spread the word.

Groups of children gathered to take their campaign on the road.

The children called out something, and the woman laughed. The knot in Maggie's stomach was still tight, but her father pressed a smile onto his face, and Maggie chose that moment to escape out the back with her deliveries.

"Why aren't you out here with us?" snooty Jennifer asked. Maggie had tried to sneak her bike around the side of the store, but Jennifer had spotted her.

"I'm protesting later," Maggie said. "Somewhere else."

"Yeah," Charlie said, "she can't strike against her own father."

"But she doesn't have to *work* for him," Jennifer said and stuck out her tongue.

Maggie was so shocked that she didn't know what to say at first. Then her temper flared. "What do you know about it?" she demanded. "You get everything served to you on a silver platter. And why is my dad the enemy? *He* didn't make chocolate prices go up."

"Do you see any five-cent candy bars in there?" Jennifer taunted her, pointing at the front door of the shop. She made a noise as if she'd stepped in dog doodoo. "So much for solidarity."

"What's solirarity, Jennifer?" asked a boy who barely reached her shoulder.

"Soli*da*rity," she corrected him. "It means you stick together. It means you don't work for someone who's selling chocolate bars at eight cents when you should be out protesting."

"I told you, I'm going protesting later," Maggie argued. "And if you knew the first thing about having to earn a living, you'd know that he *can't* sell his chocolate bars for less. He'd lose money. And that's not just about candy. That's about having food on the table."

Jennifer spun on her heel and shouted her slogan into the street. "Eight-cent bars can go to hang. *I'm* one of the gang."

Maggie jumped on her bicycle and took off, shaking with anger. Jennifer *wasn't* one of the gang. No one liked her, except for the presents she gave for birthdays, and her stupid slogan wasn't even catchy. The bad part was that, apparently, Maggie was no longer part of the gang either, just because she was working for her own father, to buy a birthday present for her best friend.

She pedaled away as fast as she could, trying to think about the excitement of the protest. She didn't want to think about her father, and the store, and how hopeless her birthday plans were becoming.

All through her deliveries, Maggie's stomach was not quite right. She felt even worse when she got home, picked up her protest sign, and snuck out of the yard without her father seeing her.

Jo was already on the front steps of McNally's Grocery when Maggie pulled up on her bicycle. She'd had to pedal all the way past the Legislature Buildings, past the Empress Hotel, and partway along Government Street. This was as far as she could get from home without her parents saying she was too far away, and she was glad the trip was over.

"We don't care the price of a car! We want a 5-cent candy bar!"

"Sorry I'm late," she told Jo. "Jennifer is protesting at Dad's store, and she made a big fuss, saying that I don't care about chocolate and that I shouldn't work for him anymore."

Jo sighed. She was about to say something when a man in a suit and tie climbed the steps of the grocery store.

"You're not planning on buying a candy bar, are you, sir?" Jo asked, looking up at him.

"I don't know," said the man, rubbing at an invisible stain on his sleeve. "Why *shouldn't* I buy a candy bar?" He smiled, as though he'd found a question Jo couldn't answer.

"Because we're *boycotting* eight-cent candy bars," Jo explained, saying the big word slowly so that he'd understand. "Only a boycott can drive prices down."

He chuckled and pulled open the shop door. "Well, maybe I'll settle for chewing gum, then."

At least he was willing to help. In the hour that the girls spent in front of McNally's, Maggie saw through the shop window that a few women slipped eight-cent candy bars into their pockets before passing the protesters. Most people, though, cheered and waved as they walked or drove past Jo's and Maggie's signs. Several congratulated them on their hard work. One woman brought them each a glass of lemonade on a tray.

"Maybe by my birthday," Jo said, "the strike will be over, and you and I can split a bar."

Maggie nodded her head vigorously, but she couldn't imagine eating part of Jo's birthday present after working so hard to get it.

By the time they saw Charlie on his way home from protesting at another store, Maggie was tired and hungry, and all this talk of chocolate didn't help. But Charlie had an idea so exciting that it almost made her forget about food.

"Why don't we have a parade?" he suggested.

"A parade," gasped Jo. "Could we?"

"Why not?" asked Charlie. "We have lots of people and signs, and we can think of other things to put in it too."

Maggie thought a parade was a great idea. It would lead the protesters away from the stores and into the streets. "Maybe I'll decorate my bike, if I have time," she said. "When would the parade be? Tomorrow?"

"No, we need a few days to prepare," said Charlie. "How about Saturday?"

Maggie's heart sank. Saturday was the day *after* Jo's birthday. "You think we'll still be boycotting eight-cent candy bars on Saturday?"

"Who knows?" said Charlie. "Maybe, by then, it'll be a victory parade."

"I sure hope so," said Maggie.

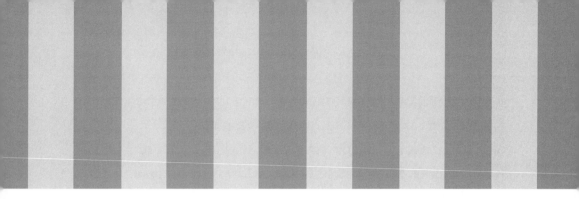

Chapter 8
We Mean Business

Maggie was even more exhausted by the time she got home, and she hoped her mother was making something warm and yummy for supper.

Even before she opened the apartment door, she heard Thomas's voice raised.

"It's not about the *shopkeepers*."

"I know that," their father said, "but—"

Maggie stepped in, and they both turned to look at her.

"Hi," she said, as if she had no idea what they were talking about. Her mother came out from the kitchen and kissed them each on the cheek. As Maggie untied her shoes, she sniffed the air, trying to guess what was for supper, but no aromas wafted in their direction. Supper must be something cold. Maybe potato salad, her favorite. Her tummy was rumbling.

On the kitchen table sat a large stack of lettuce and tomato sandwiches. Maggie and her father frowned, disappointed.

"Busy day?" he asked.

"Extremely." Maggie's mother's face was glowing, as if someone had just given her a magnificent present. "I thought the collective meeting would take an hour, but it lasted three hours. We decided to write to our MLA about the butter prices. We may start a petition, too."

"What's this RMLA?" asked Maggie.

Her father looked puzzled for a moment and then laughed. "*Our* MLA, Maggie—our Member of the Legislative Assembly. That's the person who represents us in the provincial government. Your mother wants the government to do something about these food prices." He sat down at the table and sighed, then looked up at Maggie's mother.

"At least *you're* not putting the blame on the shopkeepers."

Maggie expected her mother to lean over and kiss her father on the head, as she often did when sales slowed down. Instead, her mother slid into the seat next to him and said, "No one's blaming you, George. And the protesters aren't doing any harm. If they can't afford the prices, they won't buy from you anyway."

Like Maggie's friends, lots of children protested in front of local stores, hoping to persuade customers to join their ban on 8-cent bars.

Maggie sensed an oncoming argument, but she was too hungry to leave the table. She tucked into her sandwich and snuck a glance at her brother. He looked as though he wanted to disappear too.

"I don't know," their father said, frowning so much that his forehead became four thick wrinkles. "Protesting in the streets and writing letters to politicians is one thing. Protesting in front of my store is something else. These kids are driving my customers away."

Maggie's mother thought for a few seconds. "People who want to buy will still buy," she said. "And if you support the young protesters on your doorstep, you're likely to win customers for life."

Silence stretched out between Maggie's parents, and Maggie couldn't look at either one of them. Her mother was right, she thought, but she couldn't help feeling sorry for her dad. He'd always been so nice to the kids, and now they were protesting right in his face.

As soon as Thomas had popped the last bit of sandwich into his mouth, he jumped up from the table and asked to be excused. "I have a protest meeting over at the Five-and-Dime downtown," he announced, and their father frowned even more.

"I have to go too," Maggie whispered, eyes down.

"I can't believe that children of mine would drive away customers from innocent shopkeepers, and—"

Maggie's mother cut him off. "Have fun," she said, standing to bring her own plate to the kitchen sink. "You show them what you're made of."

What *was* she was made of, Maggie wondered, as she clomped down the stairs. She was a bit upset and uncomfortable but, with her mother's support, a little excited, too.

"So here's the plan, everyone. Pay attention."

Maggie didn't know the boy who was talking. He was one of the bigger kids, probably in grade ten or eleven. He had on a tweed cap, like the kids in the movies who sold newspapers. He pulled the cap low over his eyes, as though he didn't want to be recognized, but he was yelling so loud that surely the whole neighborhood heard him.

Maggie and Thomas had pedaled to the meeting together, past the Legislature Buildings and the Empress, along the waterfront, almost to Chinatown. Thomas kept yelling for her to hurry up, but they arrived on time anyway.

The Five-and-Dime was closed already. The adults had gone home for the evening, and the street was swarming with kids.

All day, at school, Maggie had heard whispers. "Have you heard about the meeting? Are you going?"

Jo couldn't come because she had to look after her brothers, but Thomas, Jeffrey, Jennifer, Charlie, and at least fifty other kids were there. Some wore frayed, faded clothes, and others wore expensive outfits and bright, polished shoes. All of them listened to the tall boy in the newspaper cap.

"There are meetings like this happening all over Victoria tonight," he shouted. "The protests in front of the stores are going well, and some storekeepers are trying to figure out how to get the prices down. But it's not the shopkeepers who decide the price of chocolate."

Maggie glared at Jennifer and would have stuck her tongue out, but Jennifer wasn't paying attention. She was talking to a girl next to her.

"We need to tell the whole country how we feel about the price hike," the boy in the cap shouted. "The politicians need to know how we feel, so tomorrow...tomorrow we protest at the *Legislature!*"

After a moment of astonished silence, the street burst into cheers, and suddenly everyone was talking at once.

"Will they let us in?"

"Of course not, silly. But we'll force our way in. We have to talk to the politicians, and they won't pay attention to a bunch of kids standing out on the lawn, signs or no signs."

"I'm not thure my parenth will let me," said a small boy with a lisp.

"Don't tell them, then," someone else suggested.

Maggie tugged on Thomas's sleeve. "Are you telling Mom and Dad?"

"I dunno. Probably. Mom's spending more time organizing butter protests than making our suppers now, so she'd be the last one to complain."

"Dad's not going to like it," Maggie said. "You can't just barge into the government building like that. It's probably illegal or something."

"It's not like we'll damage anything," Charlie argued. "We just want to talk to them."

Jennifer was about to put in her two cents' worth, but Maggie turned her back.

The boy in the tweed cap was still shouting to the crowd. "Tomorrow, on the lawn in front of the Legislature, as soon as school's out. We'll show them we mean *business*!"

Again, everyone cheered. Between this and the parade on Saturday, this was going to be the most exciting week ever!

The crowd dispersed, noisy and bubbling with plans.

Thomas sped home way ahead of Maggie, and by the time she put her bicycle away, he had already disappeared into the apartment. Outside the door, she listened to see what the weather was like inside. No raised voices. No whispering that she could hear. She pulled open the door.

Thomas was drinking a cup of water at the kitchen sink. The radio was playing softly in the background, and their mother was sewing Jo's blue birthday dress at the table. Maggie hugged her, and her brother cranked up the news.

"Listen! We made it onto the radio!"

Across the city again today, the broadcaster said, *children raised placards against the eight-cent candy bar. Protests started three days ago in Ladysmith and are rapidly spreading across the country. Young protesters hope that their boycott will soon return the five-cent price tag to their favorite treat.*

Maggie felt a surge of hope at their success so far. By Friday, prices just *might* come down, so that she wouldn't have to think up another birthday present for Jo after all.

Thomas cheered. "Wait till we storm the Legislature!" he said, his eyes fiery and his hands gripping an imaginary gun.

"Thomas, you're not storming anywhere," their mother said. "You're just going to ask politely what the politicians are planning to do."

Thomas ran around the kitchen, shouting, "Watcha gonna do, buster?" and he took off down the hall.

Maggie found her father in the living room. He sat in the green armchair with the daily paper spread across his lap. Maggie perched on the edge of the sofa. "Dad? I won't be home right after school for the next few days."

He looked up at her, wary, seemingly waiting for an explanation.

"I'm . . ." She hesitated. "I'm helping Mrs. Sampson." It was sort of true. Mrs. Sampson had asked her to clean the blackboards on Wednesdays this month. But that wouldn't take more than twenty minutes. And that was only tomorrow. She hoped her father wouldn't ask too many questions.

"I had a few more deliveries lined up for you in the afternoons," he said.

"I'll be back by four-thirty. I can do them then." She tried to look as confident and responsible as possible. She pushed her smile so big that his face brightened too.

"Well, I'm certainly not going to ask you to come home from school early to run errands for the shop. We're not that hard up yet."

Behind her smile, Maggie suddenly felt like crying. He was being so nice, and she was hiding things from him. But how could she tell him the whole truth?

Why did everything have to be so *complicated*?

Chapter 9
The Most Unusual Strike on Record

The next day, everyone was so excited about the Legislature protest that it was hard to concentrate on sums and spelling. The whole class was relieved when Mrs. Sampson clapped her hands twenty minutes before lunchtime and said, "You can put your books away now, children. It's time for some news."

Maggie loved the twenty minutes before lunch. Each day, students brought in newspaper clippings or told news stories they had heard on the radio. Most of the kids had heard that morning's broadcast.

Signs of revolt over rising prices are spearheaded by the Dominion's small fry, the radio announcer had declared. *They say candy sellers are sabotaging the sweet tooth and what this country needs most is a good five-cent chocolate bar. Across the country, over a hundred leaders of the lollipop brigade charge that the higher prices are unfair to Canada's candy chewers, so they've staged the most unusual strike on record.*

That broadcast left everyone talking about chocolate.

"The radio said protests are spreading across the country," Jo told the class. "Yesterday, they talked about kids in Regina, Saskatchewan. They're all on strike too. And even kids in little towns are getting on their bicycles and riding up and down the main street with signs, showing how they feel."

"What do you think will happen next?" Mrs. Sampson asked the class.

"We'll storm the Legislature, and the government will fall!" shouted Jimmy, waving a fist in the air.

"Oh, Jimmy," said Mrs. Sampson. "I heard that you were going to protest calmly and respectfully."

"Yes, Mrs. Sampson," he agreed, disappointed.

"I think it's really important to treat the situation with respect," Mrs. Sampson said. "Remember our talk about freedom and civil rights last week? In some countries, people aren't allowed to say what they think. In some places, people are *killed* if they disagree with the government."

Maggie and Jo exchanged a look. Surely not...

"Not here, of course," Mrs. Sampson assured them. "But

it's still important to exercise our freedom without being disrespectful."

"But Mrs. Sampson," said George, who sat in the back row. "The government's not respecting *us*."

The teacher nodded slowly. "Just try to remember, all of you, that this isn't a personal attack. During the war, and just after, the government gave extra money to the manufacturers to help them stay in business. If it hadn't been for that money, there wouldn't be any chocolate to buy."

"See?" Jennifer whispered to Jimmy.

"I beg your pardon?" asked Mrs. Sampson, giving her a sharp look.

Jennifer sat up very straight in her chair. "I was just saying, Mrs. Sampson, that if it weren't for the government, we wouldn't have chocolate at all, so why should we attack them?"

"Who's attacking the government?" Maggie asked. "We just want to tell them how we feel. They can't be a good government if they don't know how people feel."

At that moment, the bell rang, and the class was dismissed. Maggie found her lunch box over by the coat racks and looked for Jo, who was talking to Jennifer.

"Hey Jennifer," Maggie said. "How come yesterday you said mean things to me about being a traitor, and now you don't want to protest in front of the Legislature?"

"Her dad works there," Jo said.

"*Oh*," said Maggie, as if she didn't know this already. "So he's one of the people who control the prices, then?"

"No," Jennifer said. "He has nothing to do with it, and I don't see why you should pick on him."

"No one's picking on him," Jo said. "We're just saying what we think."

Jennifer frowned. "Well, don't you forget what Mrs. Sampson said. People in some countries get killed for saying what they think, and you'd better be thankful to have such a good government." She spun around and marched away, leaving Jo and Maggie to look at each other and shake their heads.

⊶⊷ ⊶⊷ ⊶⊷

That afternoon, the kids poured out of the school and down the hill to the Legislature Buildings, waving their signs. Their school was closer than any other, and they got there first, but they didn't have to wait very long before other children flooded the lawn too. Within half an hour, more than two hundred kids were marching and shouting, making such a racket that a man in a blue uniform poked his head out of the front door.

"Five cents is common sense!" Jo shouted toward the buildings.

"We want five-cent bars!" shouted Maggie.

"Let's go talk to the government!" called the boy in the newsboy cap. The whole crowd shifted, and Maggie laughed nervously as she felt herself swept toward the big, stone building along with everyone else. They pushed open the doors and flowed into the bright, polished halls.

"What are you going to do about chocolate prices?" the boy in the cap demanded of the first man they saw.

"How do I know?" The security guard stood with his hands on his hips in front of the rotunda, blocking their path. "I'm just supposed to keep you out of here!"

"Too late!" called Maggie, and the crowd surged past, up the stairs with the stained glass windows, toward the gallery.

As they moved, other men and a few women jumped back to watch from the doorways. Jo asked a man in a suit what he planned to do about the price hike, and Maggie barely caught his answer as she sailed by: "Uh, um, well now, I guess we'll have to give that some thought. Er...are you supposed to be in here?"

More security guards were coming now, and janitors, and up ahead someone was shouting, and the kids in front paused and began to back up. Soon the whole crowd was retreating down the stairs, cheering as they poured out of the building. The adults were shaking their heads but smiling, and Maggie was both proud of what they'd done and relieved it was over.

They must have done a good job of being respectful if everyone looked so happy.

"This way, everyone!" Thomas called. "A photographer wants to take our picture!"

Children, signs, and bicycles crammed onto the front steps of the large stone building.

Maggie whispered to Jo, "Dad told me that this is where they take pictures of *really important* visitors."

As the crowd shouted, "We want five-cent bars," the photographer snapped one picture after another.

Chapter 10
Spoiled

The next morning, Maggie flew into the kitchen with her dress barely buttoned up. "What does the news say today? Did they mention the Legislature? Have the chocolate prices come down?"

Her mother was stirring the breakfast porridge. "They mentioned the Legislature, all right. More than two hundred kids! I wish I could have been there!"

"And the prices?" Maggie asked, tugging her dress into place.

Her mother shook her head. "They haven't budged."

Maggie felt tears prick her eyes. Tomorrow, Jo would be turning ten, and Maggie didn't have a thing to give her.

"These things take time, Maggie Munchkin, but think of all you've achieved already." Her mother counted them off on her fingers: new friends, solidarity, adult support...

Maggie shook her head. She couldn't give any of *that* to Jo for her birthday.

"There I am! Back there on the left! That's me!"

Clusters of students poured over clippings from that morning's newspaper. Everyone was pressed in close, trying to spot themselves in the photo, or to point themselves out to their friends. Almost everyone was cheering and shouting excitedly.

Everyone except Maggie, that is. Nothing was going right for her that day. Her pencil broke halfway through her arithmetic quiz, and she had to spend so much time sharpening it that she almost didn't finish the test. Jo wasn't around at lunch, because she had track-and-field practice, and in the afternoon Maggie was so fed up with trying to think of another good present that she was mad right until the three o'clock bell rang.

"I'm in the perfect mood for a protest," she told Jo as they marched to McNally's Grocery with their signs. "I can't believe the price hasn't budged. If two hundred kids in the Legislature didn't change things, then what will?"

Jo sighed, hoisting her sign a little higher on her shoulder. "It's just not fair. At least we're doing something, though. We're giving it our best shot. Mom says that's what counts."

Maggie did feel better that afternoon, carrying her sign around and waving to all the people who greeted them or honked their horns as they went by. Jo didn't talk about her cousin Annette all afternoon, and Maggie was in a good mood by the time she started to pack up her things.

"Where are you going?" Jo asked. It was a quarter past four, well before stores closed, but Maggie was heading home. "Dad's expecting me," she explained. "He said I could stay out after school, but only until four-thirty. If I get my deliveries done fast enough, though, maybe I can come back."

"Don't bother!" Jo hollered her eight-cent protests extra-loud and then whipped around to face Maggie. "You don't care about this protest at all, do you? All you care about is making money."

Maggie blinked and stared at her friend.

"You're just like your dad," Jo added.

"What?"

"You heard me," Jo snapped. "He pretended he was every-one's friend, but as soon as they announced the price change, he started selling at eight cents."

"Don't you say bad things about my father!" Maggie

whispered, to avoid exploding. "He can't change the candy-bar prices. We have to eat too, you know."

"He didn't have to raise the prices right away, if he still had candy bars," Jo said.

Maggie was too furious to listen, but she refused to make a scene here in the street, where any one of her father's customers could see her. She would not be a spoiled brat like Jo. "You, Josephine Martin, are the most impossible person I've ever met!" Maggie grabbed her bike and pedaled away as fast as she could, clutching her *I can't afford an 8¢ bar* against her shoulder. Jo shouted something after her, but Maggie was too far off to hear what it was.

When Maggie got home and her dad handed her half a dozen eggs and a loaf of bread, she felt a little bit better. Pedaling was like medicine for anger. She placed the brown packages carefully into the delivery basket and got on her bicycle.

"Maggie?" her mother called from the kitchen window upstairs. "Could you stop by Mrs. Martin's house on your way? Tell her that Josephine's birthday dress is all ready, and she can pick it up any time."

Maggie groaned, but she said she would do it.

After delivering the groceries, Maggie stood in front of the last customer's house, dreading what she had to do next. The more she thought about Jo, the angrier she got. Finally she jumped on her bike again, determined not to let horrible Jo ruin her day. Besides, if she pedaled fast enough, she'd get to Jo's house and escape again before Jo got home from protesting.

Sure enough, Jo wasn't there. "She came back from protesting," Mrs. Martin said, when Maggie knocked on the door, "but Jennifer Saunders came by and invited her to a picnic."

Jennifer Saunders? Jo thought Jennifer was as snooty as Maggie did. At least, that was how Jo had felt the day before.

"Josephine's really missed you lately," Mrs. Martin said, and glanced back over her shoulder toward a clamor in the kitchen. "She helps me out with the little kids, but she needs time off, with somebody her own age. She's been terribly mopey, with you always too busy to play with her."

Maggie picked at a hangnail, feeling that Mrs. Martin expected her to apologize, but what for? Jo was the one acting like a spoiled brat, and all because Maggie was earning money for her birthday gift.

Someone inside the house burst into sobs.

"Oh-oh. I'm sorry, Maggie," Mrs. Martin said. "I've got to go. I'll tell Josephine you came by, though."

"The dress," Maggie said, suddenly remembering why she had come. "Mom said you can pick it up this evening."

"Oh, that's great, Maggie. Thanks."

Maggie pedaled away slowly. *Jo misses me,* she thought. *She's lonely*. That explanation of Jo's weirdness—and her sudden inter-est in picnics with Jennifer!—had never occurred to her.

Why so glum, Maggie?" her mother asked. She was cooking up a big pot of vegetable soup, and she'd told Maggie that there was potato salad in the fridge. Maggie was so relieved not to be eating sandwiches again that she set the table without being asked, but she couldn't stop frowning about Jo. Maggie had never meant to make her friend mopey or angry, but how could she explain what she was doing? What if Jo didn't believe her? And if Jo really wasn't a spoiled brat after all, then Maggie still wanted to give her a birthday present—but she had nothing to give.

When her mother asked what was wrong, Maggie didn't know where to start. "Dad's not going to be happy because the protest is still not over," she said finally. As she spoke, she remembered that she hadn't told either of her parents about the big parade on Saturday—and that was the day after tomorrow! But all that felt like the least of her worries right now.

"He'll live," her mother said. "You shouldn't feel bad about demanding your rights, Maggie. It's your responsibility as a citizen of a democracy to say what you think."

Maggie sighed and wondered aloud why her dad couldn't see it that way.

"Maybe you should ask him." Her mother looked at the clock by the stove. "He's still in the shop, but it's closing soon, and supper won't be ready for another forty-five minutes."

Maggie shrugged. Maybe she *would* talk to her father. Something Jo had said earlier was bouncing around in her brain and wouldn't let her think about anything else.

Maggie left the apartment and tiptoed down the stairs. She wanted to look in the back window of the shop first, to see if her father was in a good mood, before she went in.

From the back, Maggie could see across the store and through the front windows to the street. The protesters were still marching up and down and waving their signs. Her father was with a customer—old Mr. Roberts, with the stick-up-everywhere hair and a scratchy-looking face.

"Children nowadays have no respect! My father would have had my hide if I'd carried on like that."

"I don't know, Mr. Roberts. What with the war and all, they've been short on treats for as long as most of them can remember. I can understand them being upset."

Mr. Roberts grumbled some more and made his way to the door. Maggie's father followed to lock up behind him. It was six o'clock, closing time, and the protesters were leaving, too. Her father waved through the glass, and the kids waved back, smiling.

Then he spotted Maggie and realized that she'd overheard. "That's right, I do have some sympathy," he told her. "But remember that I haven't sold a single candy bar since all this nonsense started."

"It's not nonsense, Dad," Maggie said, with boldness that surprised even her. "It's important to say what we think. Like when the school picnic got canceled, and Mrs. Sampson told us that we had the power to get it back."

Maggie's father looked at her as though she'd suddenly grown a foot taller. "And here I thought you were just following the others."

"Kind of," she admitted, thinking hard about what she wanted to say next. "It's Jo's birthday tomorrow," she said finally. Her chocolate-bar secret had gotten her into so much trouble lately that it was time to let it out. "I wanted to buy her a candy bar, but then I broke the eggs, and then the price of chocolate went up, and now she's mad at me because I'm always too busy to play."

Maggie's father looked as pained as when the protesters had

first marched in front of his store. Maggie took a deep breath and told herself to be convincing, not whiny. "What I mean is, it's *important* to me, the price of chocolate. I feel bad about protesting, because you always get mad about it, but it's not our fault the prices are going up."

"Oh Maggie," said her father, leaning back against the counter and resting a hand on her shoulder. "I know it's not your fault, but it's not my fault either."

Maggie nodded. Now was the moment to ask him about what Josephine had said. Her heart beat so loud that she was convinced he could hear it, but she spoke anyway. "How much are you selling those candy bars for?" she asked, pointing to the chocolate shelf.

He frowned. "Look, I'll give you one if you want it that badly."

Maggie shook her head. "I mean, aren't those candy bars left over from before the price change? If you didn't buy them for more, then why are you selling them for more?"

"It's not that simple, Maggie," he said with a sigh. "Sure, I could sell these ones at five cents, but once the eight-cent ones come in, I won't be able to keep my prices down and still stay in business."

"I know that," Maggie said. "But if you *got* these ones at the same old price, shouldn't you *sell* them at the same old price?"

"But what about the boycott?"

"We're boycotting eight-cent candy bars, not five-cent ones. Anyone would buy for five cents, and Mom always says you should support your customers."

"It wouldn't change things for very long, Maggie."

"But in the meantime, you'd make lots of kids really happy." *Including me*, she thought. If he lowered the price, she'd buy Jo's candy bar right away, before they disappeared. "I'll make a sign for you to put in your window. I'll write, *Jenkins Grocery supports your boycott!* No—I'll write, *Kids need candy, five cents is dandy!* You'll have a million customers. By tomorrow, everyone will be talking about your shop."

For the first time in a long while, her father laughed.

"If you ever get tired of doing deliveries, kiddo, you could make your fortune in marketing."

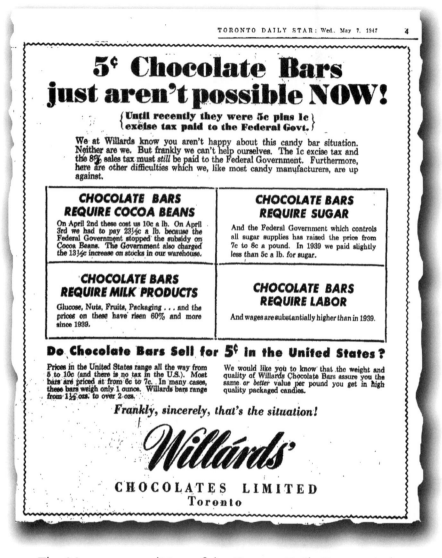

The May 7, 1947 edition of the *Toronto Daily Star* carried this ad from a chocolate manufacturer trying to explain the increase in prices.

Chapter 11
Best Friend Ever?

The next day was a fantastic Friday for Maggie. She bought the Best-Friend-Ever candy bar for Jo before putting her sign in her father's window: *Jenkins Grocery supports your boycott! Kids need candy, and 5¢ is dandy! 5¢ candy bars on sale here.*

She raced upstairs to her room and took almost everything out of her drawers, looking for something to wrap the present in. Then she spotted a bit of green paper sticking out from under the bed, and she almost got stuck under there trying to grab it, but it turned out to be the cover of a textbook she'd thought she'd lost, and she couldn't wrap Jo's present in *that*. She flew out of her room with the textbook in one hand and the chocolate bar in the other. "Mom, I need something to wrap Jo's present in!"

Her mother tied a blue hair ribbon in a big fancy bow around the candy bar. Maggie hugged her and bolted for the door. "Thank you, Mom! You saved my life!"

She pedaled as fast as she could to school, determined to talk to Jo before class started.

I'm sorry I haven't been around much lately, she practiced aloud all the way across the neighborhood. *Please don't think that I don't want us to be friends.*

But when she got there and found Jo watching her brothers on the swings, she saw Jennifer Saunders across the schoolyard, skipping toward them, and Maggie blurted her apology as fast as she could, before Jennifer got there to interfere. "I'm sorry. I don't just care about money. I wanted to buy you a chocolate bar and be the Best Friend Ever, but I couldn't until yesterday because of the boycott, and you were right about Dad's stock. He got them at the old price, and now he's only charging five cents, so I got you one. Here! Happy birthday." She thrust the chocolate bar in her friend's direction, and Jo burst out laughing, just as Jennifer arrived.

"What's so funny?" Jennifer asked, and Maggie was glad she *did* ask, because she didn't know whether Jo was laughing *at* her or *with* her.

"Maggie was trying to be the Best Friend Ever for my birthday, and I thought she just didn't like me anymore."

"What a mess!" Maggie said, not sure whether to laugh or cry.

"Like half a dozen eggs on the pavement! *Splat!*" Jo shrieked and looped her arms in both Maggie's and Jennifer's. Maggie didn't want to share Jo with Jennifer, but she was so relieved by Jo's laughter that she pretended not to care.

"Your birthday's *today?*" Jennifer asked. "You never told me! Why don't we all go to my house for ice cream after school? Maggie, you hardly ever come to my house."

Maggie decided that maybe Jennifer wasn't so bad after all.

"We can have vanilla and chocolate, and my mother might give us some peaches that she canned last summer," Jennifer said. "My mother makes the *best* canned peaches...."

As Jennifer talked about her plans, Jo closed her eyes and breathed in deep the rich, chocolaty aroma of her five-cent candy bar. "Maggie," she said, when she opened her eyes. "I didn't mean what I said about you being greedy like your father."

Maggie shrugged. "You didn't say *greedy.*"

"Didn't I? Well, I thought it," Jo admitted, looking sheepish. "But I don't think it now," she added, as they filed into the school.

Chapter 12
The Great Chocolate Parade

Saturday was pretty fantastic too. The weather was perfect, and the parade was *enormous!* Kids came from fifteen different schools, to shout out their slogans and wave their signs, and some of the banners were so big that it took two kids to carry them. A truck with a megaphone blared out slogans—*THE KIDS HAVE STARTED IT, YOU FINISH IT!* And alongside the marchers *vroomed* a real police motorcycle, holding the crowds back.

But the best part was the animals. Irene Overton was riding a beautiful Shetland pony, with a sign saying *Bring the prices down to our size.* A little boy about Will's age was riding a donkey with a sign saying *Be like the mule—stubborn—don't buy 8¢ bars.*

And some kids had brought along their dogs, dressed up with signs too.

The only bad news was that the official price of chocolate hadn't changed one bit. Still, to Jo and Maggie, this felt like a victory parade anyway. The streets were full of adults who supported them, and several shopkeepers were selling chocolate for five cents again. Kids really could make a difference.

As they marched down the street, calling out their slogans, traffic stopped at all the intersections to let them pass. People paused to watch them and clapped as they went by. Even the workers inside the buildings threw open the windows and leaned out to cheer.

"I've never seen so many kids!" Jo said, as they started down Quadra Street. "There must be three times as many as we had at the Legislature!"

"Hey, Jo," little Will said, "did you see the mule? Can we get one?" He was struggling with his sign, which was almost as big as him. His older brother Allen had carried it for him part of the way.

"And Irene's pony is so cute!" Maggie said.

"This is the best parade ever," said Jo, linking her arm through Maggie's.

At the end of the parade, their mothers met them at Thunderbird Park with cookies and lemonade. When they got home, Maggie's father announced that his youngest customers had come back, just as Maggie had said they would. "And I've already got a plan for when I run out of five-cent candy bars. I'm going to put a jar beside the cash register and call it the Five-Cent Candy Bar Fund, and my customers can make a donation to help a child buy a candy bar. So I can keep selling chocolate bars for five cents, without all of us eating porridge forever."

"Thank goodness for that!" said Thomas. He turned to Maggie, who was gathering her brown-paper parcels for a few deliveries, and he said, "I'm glad you thought of a way around the boycott, kid. You're not as dumb as you look."

Coming from Thomas, that was almost a compliment. Maggie left the shop with a big grin on her face.

The next day, Thomas burst through the apartment door early, waving a newspaper. "Look at this!" he shouted. "Look! Look! We're in the newspaper again!"

SUNDAY, MAY 4, 1947

Victoria Children, 700 Strong, March In Protest Over Chocolate Bar Prices

Nearly 700 strong, Victoria youth yesterday made it clear to all they were not giving up their fight for the return of a five-cent chocolate bar.

Massing at Central Park, the large assembly paraded in an orderly fashion through the downtown area late in the morning. Many hundreds carried big placards and banners — each strongly condemning the eight-cent bar, and calling for the "good ol' nickel" model.

Boys and girls participated. The procession, arranged and organized by the Youth Action Committee, coursed from the park along Quadra Street, to Pandora, along Pandora to Douglas, along Douglas to Thunderbird Park. Disbanding at the latter park, small groups continued the campaign throughout the city. They visited buildings and offices. More than one citizen was approached with such slogans as "Roses are red, violets are blue, we're on strike, why aren't you?"

Transfusions
By Red Cross

Thieves Enter

The Daily Colonist, Sunday May 4, 1947, page 3

85

Historical Note

The national children's strike over chocolate bars really did happen. It started in Ladysmith, British Columbia, on April 25, 1947, and spread across the country. Kids in New Brunswick pooled their sugar rations to make a huge batch of fudge, so that no one ate eight-cent candy bars. Kids in Victoria stormed the Legislature, and on May 3, kids all across the country paraded in the streets to protest the price hike.

The characters in this book are imaginary, and for dramatic reasons, I have changed the date of the storming of the Legislature from Tuesday, April 29, to Wednesday April 30. All other historical details are correct.

The strike ended abruptly on May 4, 1947, after the *Toronto Telegram* published an article claiming that children were being exploited to advance political causes. Many adults were alarmed by the possibility, and the schools withdrew their support for the protest. The strikes stopped, but not before the children achieved something remarkable. All across the country, they had made their point. Shopkeepers found ways to continue selling chocolate bars to kids for five cents, despite the new prices.

In Montreal, children protested in French and English.

'WE'LL EAT WORMS FIRST'
STUDENTS SPURN 8-CENT BAR

Special to The Star

Ottawa, May 2 — Three hundred students of Lisgar collegiate today staged a lunch-hour march through a thunderstorm to Parliament Hill, a mile away, to demand return of the five-cent chocolate bar. They carried placards bearing the words: "We'll eat worms before the eight-cent bar."

The students lined up in front of the parliament buildings chanting "We want Abbott!" and "We want Howe!" for 10 minutes. No one came out and they marched off.

Picket Vancouver Stores

Vancouver, May 2—(CP)—More than 150 housewives are picketing Vancouver stores today and officials of the Housewives' Consumer association predicted the number would be tripled in the effort to bring about reduction of prices.

The women carried placards

ONLY 5 YEARS NOW
FOR BICYCLE THEFT

Nassau, Bahamas, May 3—(CP)— Chief Justice O. L. Bancroft, who caused a mild sensation in judicial circles last year when he sentenced a man to 10 years in prison for theft of a bicycle, yesterday announced from the bench a new standard of sentences for the offence.

Anyone convicted of stealing a bicycle, he said, would receive five years if it were a first offence and 10 years for persons with a crime record.

reading: "Buyers' strike," "buy no goods today."

Must Begin at Source

Hingham, Mass., May 2—The "Newburyport plan" of 10 per cent. price reductions will be dropped after tomorrow, the Chamber of Commerce announced today, because merchants contended price reductions must originate at the source of supply.

SPEND 30 MINUTES IN...

The *Toronto Daily Star*, May 3, 1947 — Students in Ottawa vowed to eat worms before they'd eat an eight-cent bar.

Acknowledgments

Thanks to Robin Neustaeter for telling me about the chocolate protests and to Phillip Daniels for his excellent film *The Five-Cent War*, which brought the protests to life. I'm indebted to Phillip Daniels, Norma Corbett, Wendy Turnbull, Carey Pallister, Jennifer Patterson, and Gilles Leclerc for their generous research assistance. Thanks also to Norene Smiley, Jane Buss, and the wonderful women at Second Story Press for their support and encouragement. To Gastón Castaño, Alvera and Henry Mulder, and Maureen Parker, I extend an extra special thank you for being such a loyal and tireless cheering section!

Photo Credits

Photos and articles are reprinted with permission from the following sources: